The Custodian
from the
Black Lagoon

by Mike Thaler · pictures by Jared Lee

SCHOLASTIC INC.

New York   Toronto   London   Auckland   Sydney   Mexico City   New Delhi   Hong Kong

To Matthew, my son.—M.T.
To Carole Inkrott, dedicated teacher.—J.L.

visit us at www.abdopublishing.com

Reinforced library bound edition published in 2014 by Spotlight, a division of the ABDO Group, PO Box 398166, Minneapolis, MN 55439. Spotlight produces high-quality reinforced library bound editions for schools and libraries. Published by agreement with Scholastic, Inc.

Printed in the United States of America, North Mankato, Minnesota.
102013
012014

 This book contains at least 10% recycled materials.

Library of Congress Cataloging-in-Publication Data

This title was previously cataloged with the following information:

Thaler, Mike, 1936-
  The custodian from the black lagoon / by Mike Thaler ; pictures by Jared Lee.
  p. cm. -- (Black Lagoon)
  Summary: After relating all of the horrible things the school custodian, Fester Smudge, is known to have done, a student whose locker won't open needs Mr. Smudge's help.
  1. Janitors--Fiction. 2. Fear--Fiction. 3. Schools--Fiction. I. Title. II Series.
  PZ7.T3 Cu 2001
  [Fic]--dc23   2001020519

ISBN 978-1-61479-196-6 (Reinforced Library Bound Edition)

All Spotlight books are reinforced library binding
and manufactured in the United States of America.

Somewhere in the dark caverns beneath our school lurks
the custodian.
His name is Fester Smudge.

I've never seen him because he waits until everyone's gone home before he emerges.

He knows all the secret passages and tunnels beneath the school—just like the Phantom of the Opera.

They say if you ride by after dark you can hear him playing terrible tunes in his giant cave.

They say it's like Dr. Frankenstein's lab, full of machines that whirl, whizz, whirr, hum, crackle, and pop!

And in the darkest corner roars a fire-breathing dragon with big white eyes and metal teeth.

He's trained it to make the school boiling hot all summer . . .

and freezing cold all winter.
They say you can even ice skate in the halls.

Derek says Fester is mechanically challenged.

He changed a lightbulb and blew the ceiling off the gym.

Then he tried to fix a leak, and the cafeteria was underwater for a week.

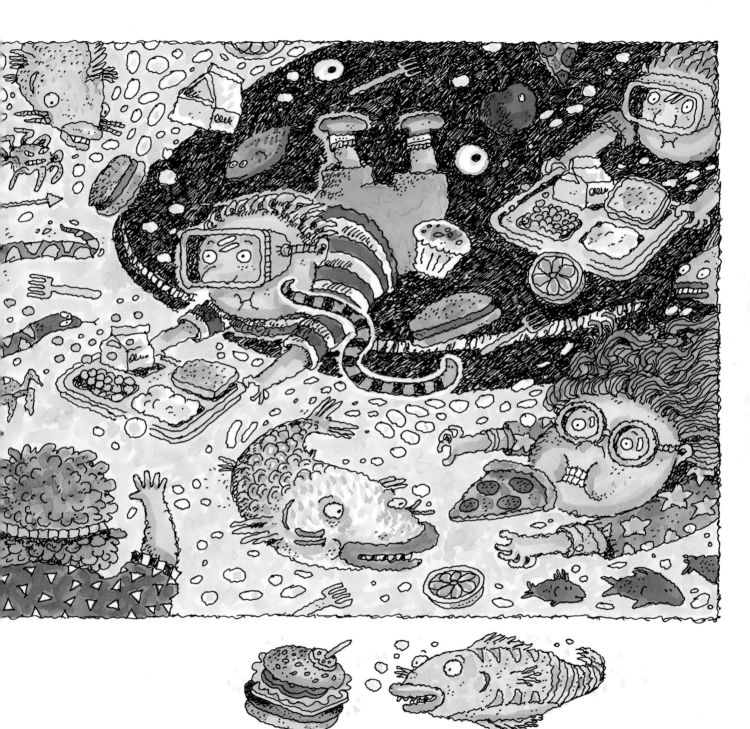

Eric says Fester's grandfather was the engineer on the *Titanic*,

and his grandmother worked on the *Hindenburg.*

Kids are still talking about the time he electrocuted a visiting author with the clip-on mike . . .

and how the fire department came to free him from a folding chair . . .

and a Coast Guard helicopter came to rescue him from a toilet bowl.

Doris says he's not a very fussy cleaner either and
our school has been designated as the town landfill.

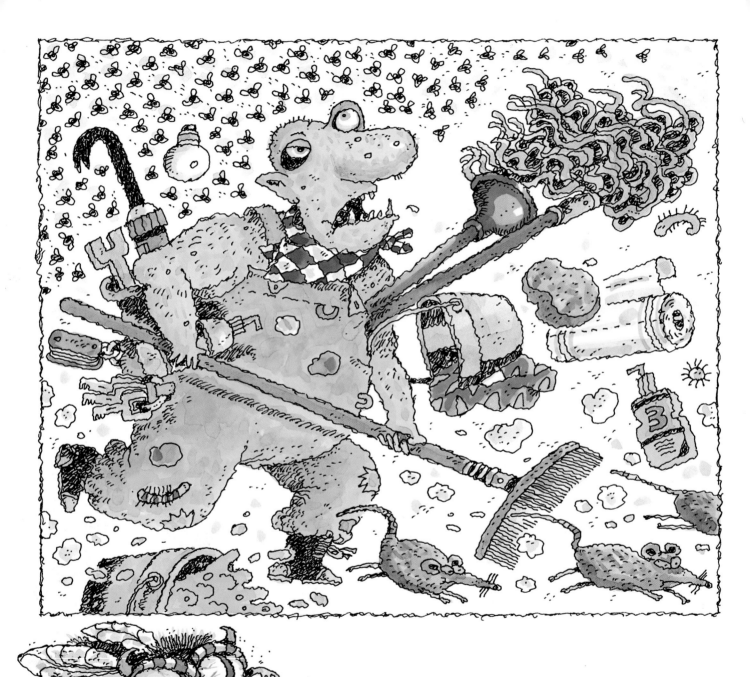

Freddy says flies follow Fester everywhere.

Kids almost saw him the time he folded up the lunch tables while everyone was still eating . . .

 or when he got his foot tangled in the rope and spent the day at the top of the flag pole.

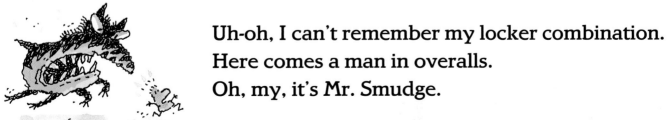

Uh-oh, I can't remember my locker combination.
Here comes a man in overalls.
Oh, my, it's Mr. Smudge.

He has lots of keys on a ring, and he opens my locker.
Then he smiles, shines the handle, and walks away whistling.

Hey, he's really neat.
I'm gonna ask him if I can see his dragon sometime.